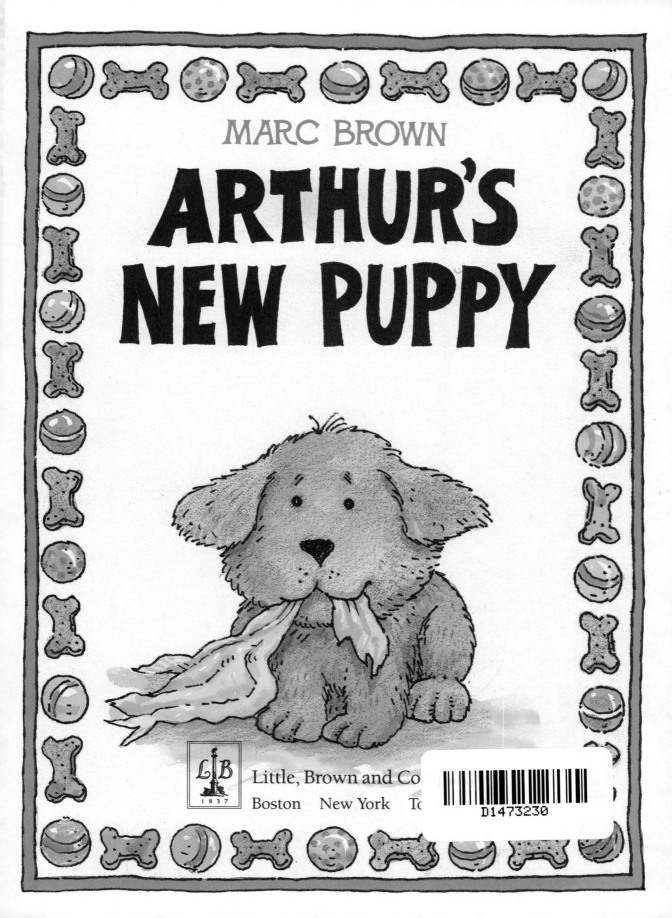

MARC BROWN

ARTHUR'S NEW PUPPY

Little, Brown and Co
Boston   New York   To

With thanks to Dorothy Crawford, the Kriegstein family,
and the lucky dogs in their lives.

Copyright © 1993 by Marc Brown

First Paperback Edition

Library of Congress Cataloging-in-Publication Data

Brown, Marc Tolon.
    Arthur's new puppy / Marc Brown.—1st ed.
         p.   cm.
    Summary: Arthur's new puppy causes problems when it tears the
living room apart, wets on everything, and refuses to wear a leash.
    ISBN 0-316-11355-7 (hc)
    ISBN 0-316-11453-7 (pb)
    [1. Dogs—Fiction.   2. Pets—Fiction.   3. Aardvark—Fiction.
4. Animals—Fiction.]   I. Title.
PZ7.B81618Arn   1993
[E]—dc20   92-46342

10 9 8 7 6 5 4 3 2

WOR

Published simultaneously in Canada
by Little, Brown & Company (Canada) Limited

Printed in the United States of America

Arthur loved his new puppy.
And Pal loved Arthur.
"He's a very active puppy," said Arthur.
"He's a very *naughty* puppy," said D.W.
"Don't worry," said Arthur. "I'll have him trained in no time."

"Here's your new home," said Arthur. "You'll have the whole garage to yourself."
But Pal did not like the garage.
As soon as Arthur put him down, Pal ran and hid.
"He feels lonesome," said Arthur. "Can he stay in the house? Please, please, please?"
"Oh, all right," said Mother, "but only for a day or two."

Arthur made a cozy spot for Pal in the kitchen.
"I thought you might need a few newspapers," said D.W.
Arthur held Pal carefully, the way his puppy book showed.
"Look, he's so excited," said Arthur.

"Look at your pants," said D.W. "You have excitement all over them."
"It's okay," said Arthur. "He's just a baby."
"Well, I think baby dogs should wear diapers," said D.W.

Later, Pal ate his dinner in a flash.
"Oh, oh," said D.W. "He has that look in his eyes again."
"Quick," said Arthur. "His leash."
But when Pal saw his leash, he ran and hid.

"I don't think he likes his leash," said D.W.
"Help me find him," said Arthur.
"I guess he didn't have to go after all," said D.W. "I was wrong."
"No, you were right," said Arthur. "He just went."

Later that night, when everyone was asleep, Pal yelped and howled until he woke up the entire family.
"Go to sleep," said Arthur.
Pal wanted to play.
"Don't forget to close his gate," called Mother.
"Good night," said Father.
"Good luck," said D.W.

The next morning Arthur was still in the kitchen. "Wake up, sleepyhead," said D.W., "and be careful where you step."
"Oh, no," said Arthur, "I forgot to close Pal's gate."
"Here's your scooper," said Mother.
"You think this is bad," said Father, "wait until you see the living room."

Pal looked very proud of himself.
"My new drapes," cried Mother.
"My doll!" screamed D.W.
"Bad dog!" said Arthur.

"Pal is moving to the garage," ordered Mother.
"Here's the key to the garage," said Father.
"I'll help you move his things after dinner."
Father put the key on the hall table.

Arthur packed up Pal's things and went to get the garage key, but it was gone.
The whole family searched for the key.
Pal watched.
"It has to be here somewhere," said Mother.
But the key was nowhere to be found.

"It looks like you can stay in the house one more night," Arthur said.

"I heard Mom and Dad whispering," said D.W., "and Pal's in big trouble. They said he better be trained soon or else!"

"Shushh!" said Arthur. "You'll hurt his feelings."

That night, Arthur remembered to close Pal's gate.

At school, Arthur told Francine and Buster about training
Pal. "I'm going to teach him to do all kinds of things!"
said Arthur.

"I used to have a puppy, too," said Buster.
"But he was too much trouble. My parents sent him to a farm."

"My cousin had a problem puppy," said Francine, "No one could train him. One day he just disappeared while she was at school."
After school Arthur hurried home.

"Oh, no!" said Arthur. "What happened?"
"I thought I'd take him for a walk," said D.W. "But when he saw the leash, he went wild! You better get this cleaned up before Mom sees it."

"Where is Mom?" asked Arthur.

"In the backyard," said D.W. "Looking for the garage key."

"Have you seen my dog-training book?" asked Arthur.

"What's left of it is over there," said D.W.

That night Arthur gave Pal an extra training lesson.
"I'll help you train this beast," said D.W. "Let me get
my whip."
"No!" said Arthur. "Dogs respond better to love."
"Watch," said Arthur. "He's getting better."
"Sit," said Arthur.

"Lie down," said Arthur.

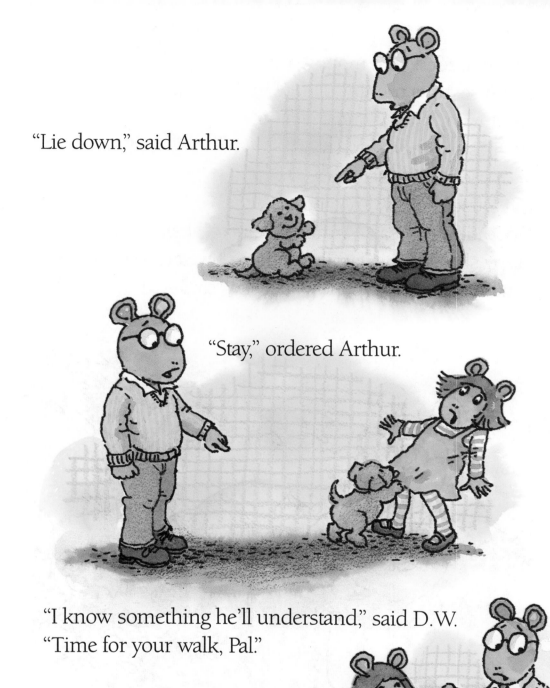

"Stay," ordered Arthur.

"I know something he'll understand," said D.W.
"Time for your walk, Pal."

"He just needs a little more work, that's all," said Arthur.

But Pal needed a lot more work.
Arthur set up a training school in the backyard.
On Monday, they worked on "sit."
On Tuesday, they worked on "down."
Wednesday was "stay" day.
By Thursday, Pal was doing tricks.
"Good dog, Pal," said Arthur. Arthur decided to put on a
puppy show for his family. "When they see how well you're
trained, they'll never send you away," said Arthur.

Arthur got up early Saturday morning to give Pal a bath.
After breakfast, Arthur's family took their seats.
"Welcome to Arthur's puppy show," said Arthur. He held
his breath. "What you are about to see will amaze and
astound you!"
"If Pal amazes us any more, our whole house
will be destroyed," said D.W.

Arthur clapped his hands.
"Come!" he said.
And Pal came.

"Sit," said Arthur.
And Pal sat.

"Down," said Arthur.
Down went Pal.

Pal even did a trick.
"Good dog!" said Arthur.

"He *is* a good dog," said Mother.

"You mean he won't have to live on a farm?" asked Arthur.

"Of course not," said Father, "not even in the garage."

No one noticed Pal run behind the rosebushes . . .

. . . when Pal returned, he sat up and wagged his tail.
"Look, he has something in his mouth," said D.W.
"It's the key to the garage!" said Arthur.
"Good boy, Pal," said Father.
"Amazing!" said Mother.

That night Arthur gave Pal a special dinner.

"Time for your walk, Pal!" said Arthur. "I'll get your leash."

But Arthur couldn't find it anywhere.

"It was on the hook a minute ago," said Arthur.

"I know I left it there."

"I'll help you look," said D.W.

Mother and Dad helped, too.

"It has to be here somewhere . . . ," said Arthur.

No one noticed Pal run behind the rosebushes.